TO:

FROM:

The 13 Days of Swiftness

A CHRISTMAS CELEBRATION FOR FANS

For Ann, Laura, Liz, Lisa, and everyone else who provided invaluable enthusiasm and insight—I'm a big fan of *you*.

—*T.G.*

Little, Brown and Company • Hachette Book Group • 1290 Avenue of the Americas, New York, NY 10104 Visit us at LBYR.com • First Edition: September 2024 • Little, Brown and Company is a division of Hachette Book Group, Inc. The Little, Brown name and logo are registered trademarks of Hachette Book Group, Inc. The publisher is not responsible for websites (or their content) that are not owned by the publisher. • Little, Brown and Company books may be purchased in bulk for business, educational, or promotional use. For information, please contact your local bookseller or the Hachette Book Group Special Markets Department at special.markets@hbgusa.com. LCCN: 2024938292 • ISBN: 978-0-316-58335-0 (paper over board) • PRINTED IN MARYLAND, USA • PHX • 10 9 8 7 6 5 4 3 2 1

The 13 Days of Swiftness

A CHRISTMAS CELEBRATION FOR FANS

BY
Tiffany Garland

ART BY
Brooke O'Neill

Little, Brown and Company
New York   Boston

On the *13ᵗʰ* day of Swiftness, my bestie shared with me:

13
selfies sleighing,

12
strings for strumming,

11

bracelets beaded,

DECEMBER

WISHING STAR

FAIRYTALE

BRAVE & WILD

♥ NYC ♥

10
boots bejeweled,

9
scrabooks sparkling,

cookies chai-spiced,

MUSIC

VACATION

7

spheres
for shaking,

6 carols chorused,

folded

rings!

4
chunky cardis,

3

cozy kitties,

2
hearts from hands,

And a *Sag** for the top of our tree!

*Sagittarius